SUPER-DRAGON

WRITTEN BY
STEVEN KROLL · DOUGLAS HOLGATE
ILLUSTRATED BY

MARSHALL CAVENDISH CHILDREN

Marshall Cavendish Corporation, 99 White Plains Road, Tarrytown, NY 10591
www.marshallcavendish.us/kids

Library of Congress Cataloging-in-Publication Data
Kroll, Steven.
Super-Dragon / by Steven Kroll ; illustrated by Douglas Holgate. — 1st ed.
p. cm.
Summary: Drago the little dragon surprises his family when he enters a
stunts flying competition with them, after taking flying lessons from a bird.
ISBN 978-0-7614-5819-7
[1. Dragons—Fiction. 2. Flight—Fiction. 3. Contests—Fiction.] I.
Holgate, Douglas, ill. II. Title.
PZ7.K9225Su 2011
[E]—dc22
2010018268

The illustrations are rendered in pencil, ink, and Photoshop.
Book design by Anahid Hamparian
Editor: Margery Cuyler

Printed in Malaysia [T]
First edition
1 3 5 6 4 2

Marshall Cavendish
Children

For Kathleen
—S.K.

For Angus and Allyson, with thanks to Mel
—D.H.

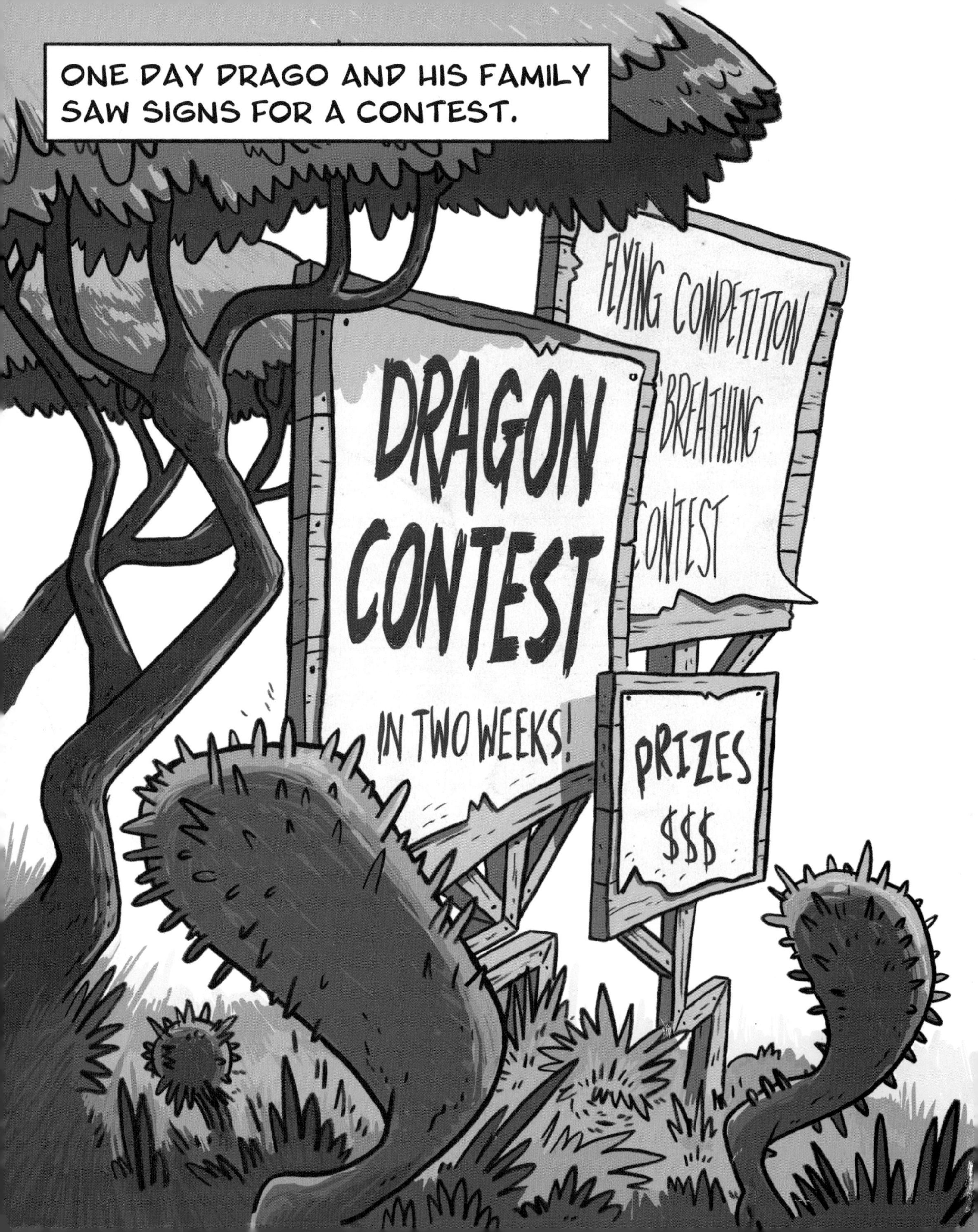
ONE DAY DRAGO AND HIS FAMILY SAW SIGNS FOR A CONTEST.
DRAGON CONTEST
IN TWO WEEKS!
FLYING COMPETITION
BREATHING
CONTEST
PRIZES
$$$

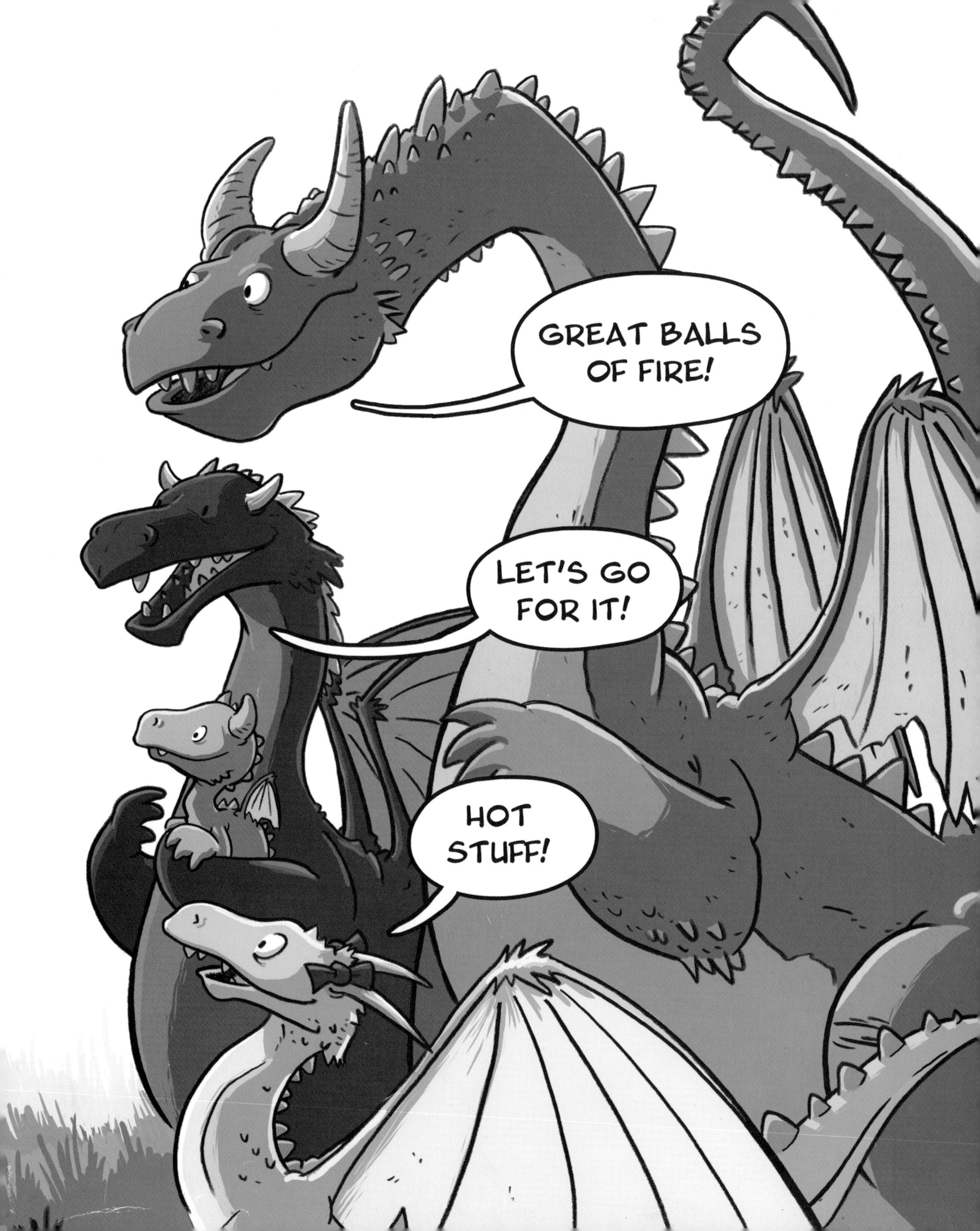
GREAT BALLS OF FIRE!
LET'S GO FOR IT!
HOT STUFF!

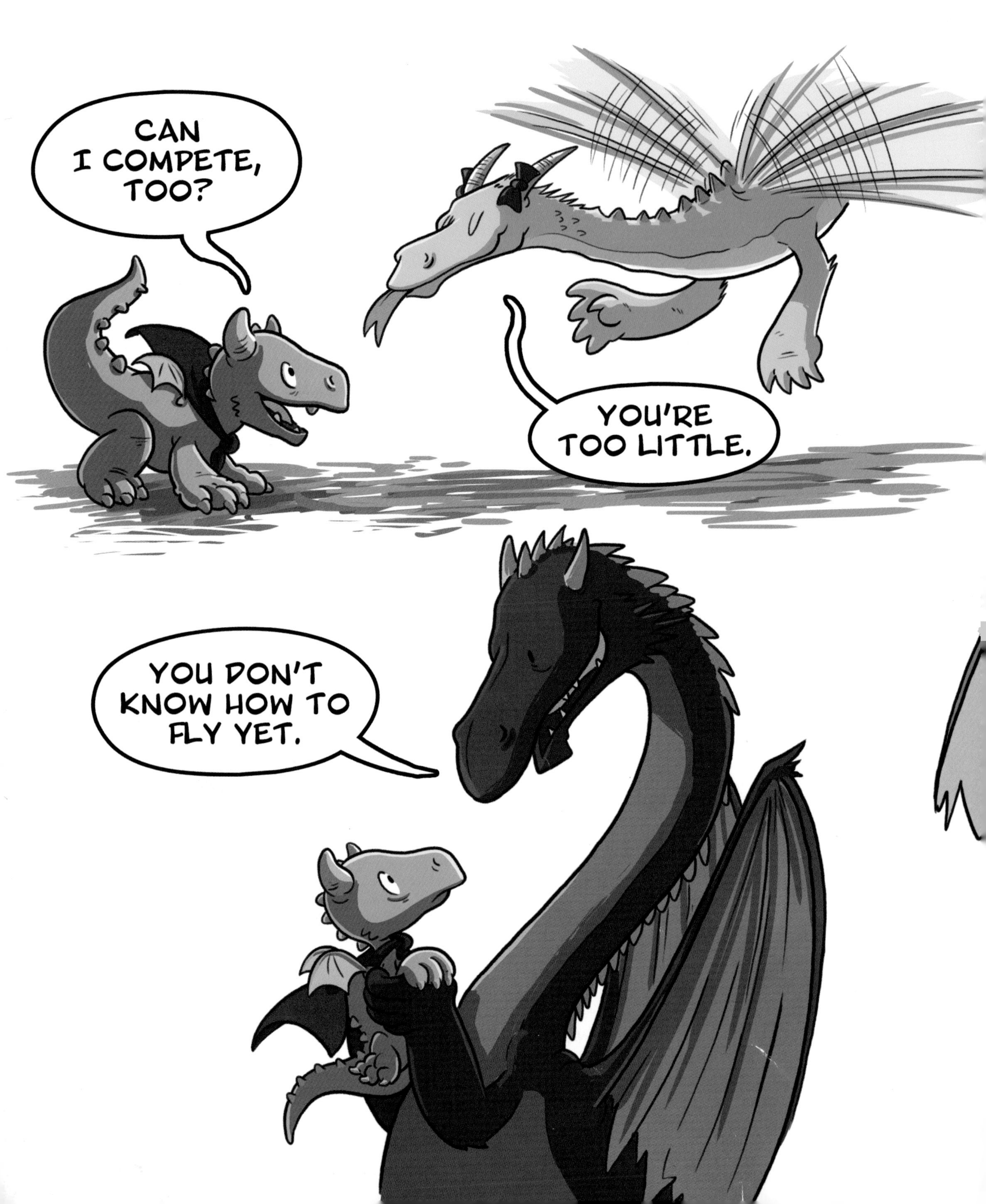
CAN I COMPETE, TOO?
YOU'RE TOO LITTLE.
YOU DON'T KNOW HOW TO FLY YET.

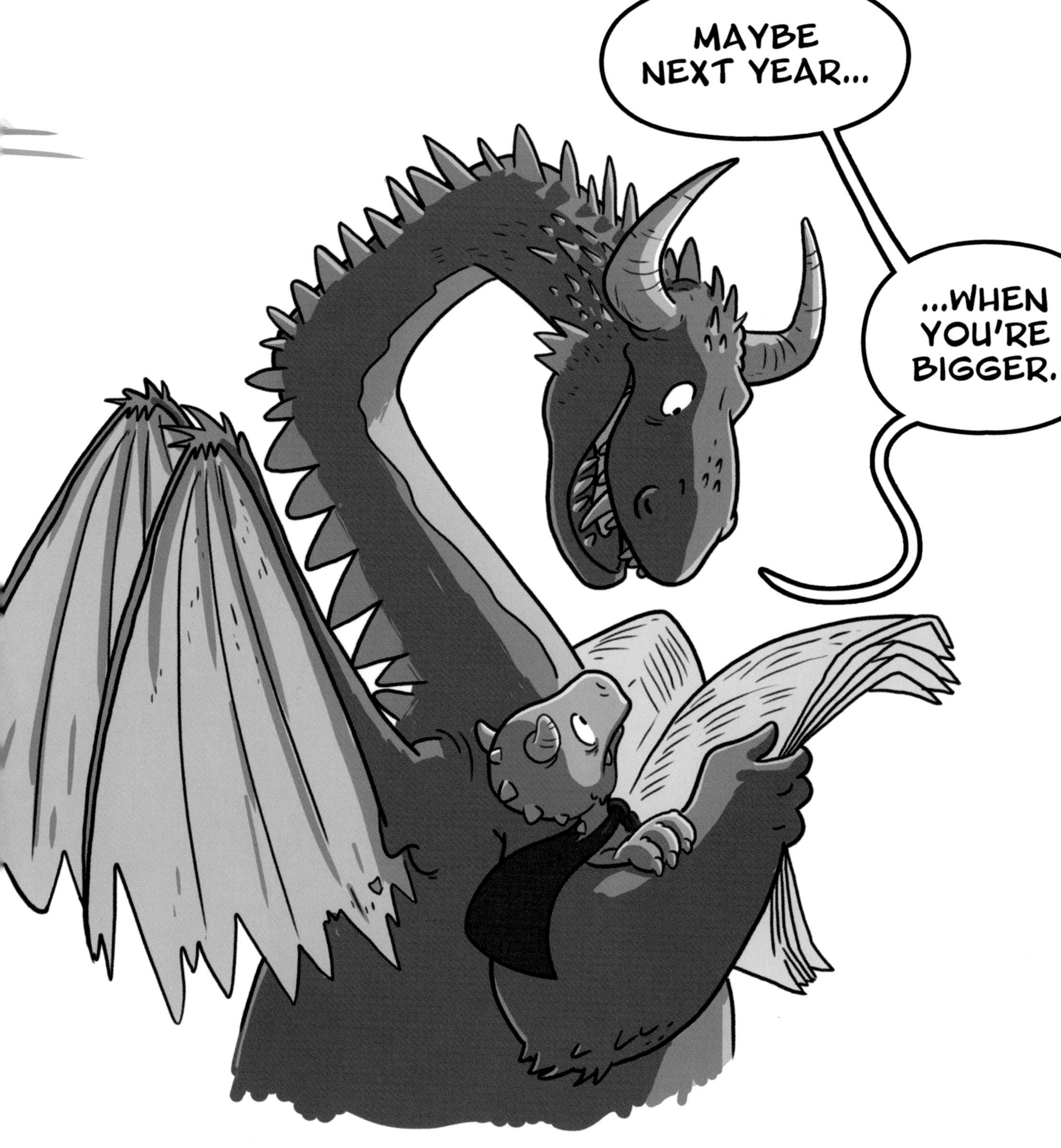
MAYBE NEXT YEAR...
...WHEN YOU'RE BIGGER.

DRAGO WAS SAD. HE WISHED HE COULD FLY.

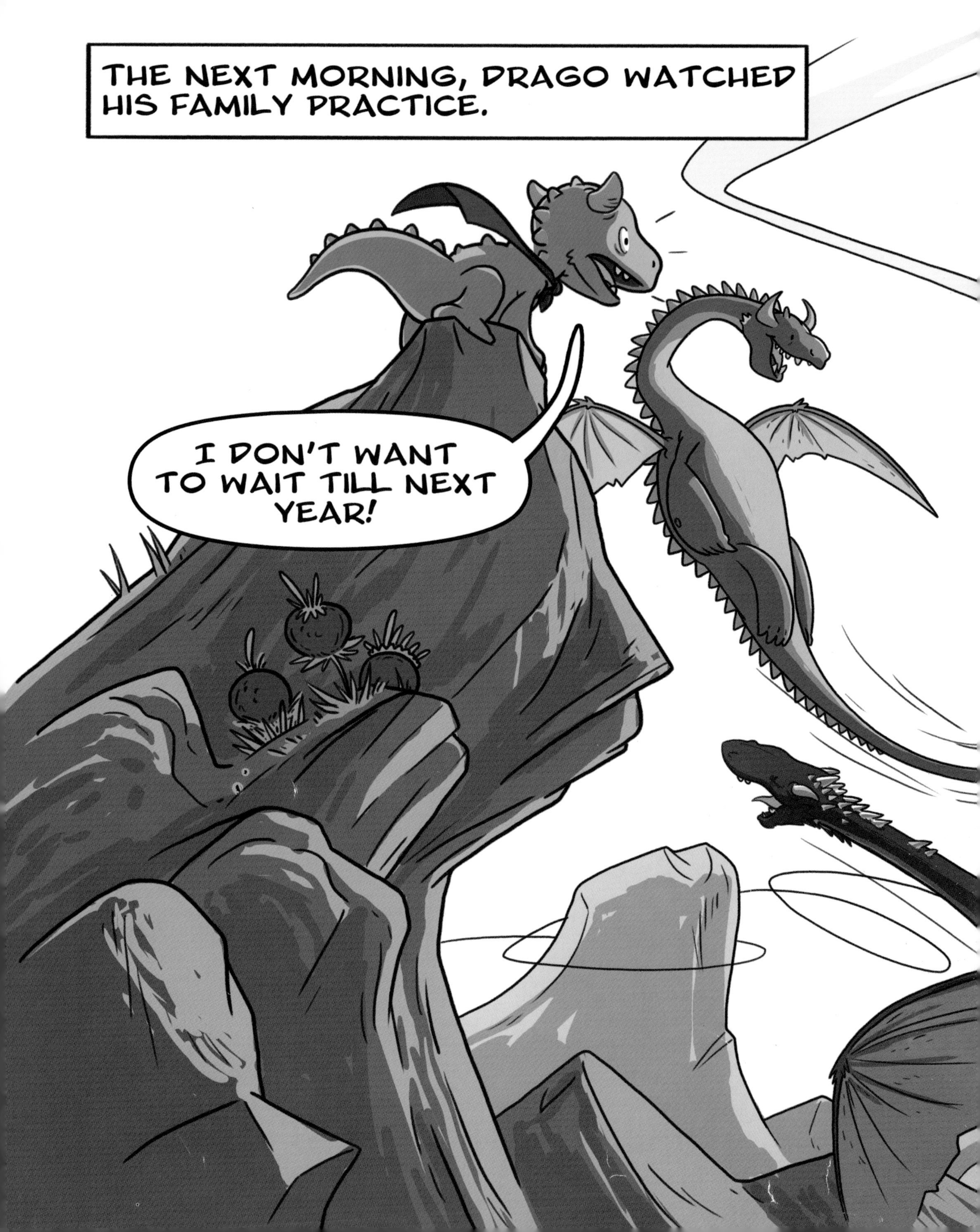
THE NEXT MORNING, DRAGO WATCHED HIS FAMILY PRACTICE.
I DON'T WANT TO WAIT TILL NEXT YEAR!

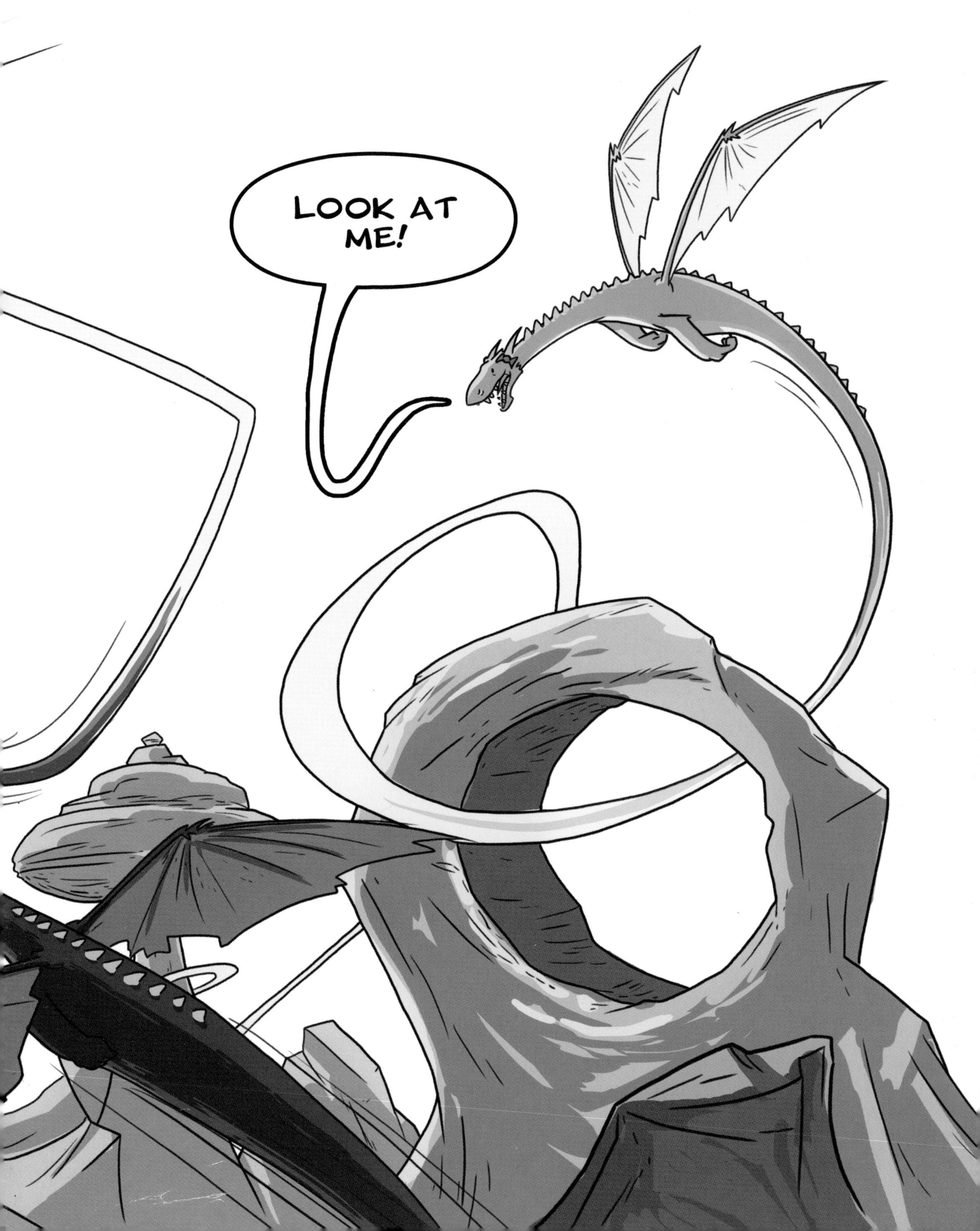
LOOK AT ME!

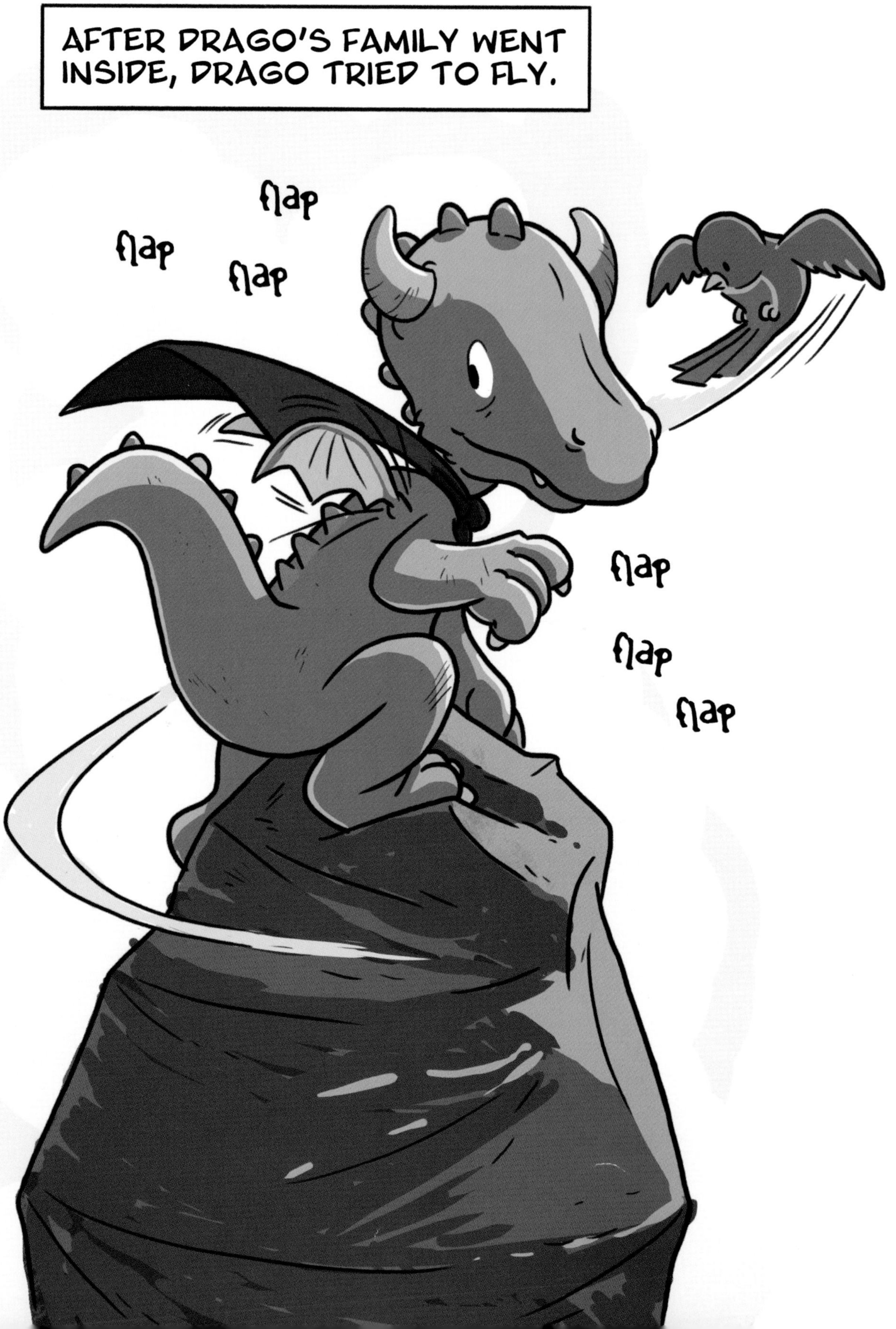
AFTER DRAGO'S FAMILY WENT INSIDE, DRAGO TRIED TO FLY.
flap
flap
flap
flap
flap
flap

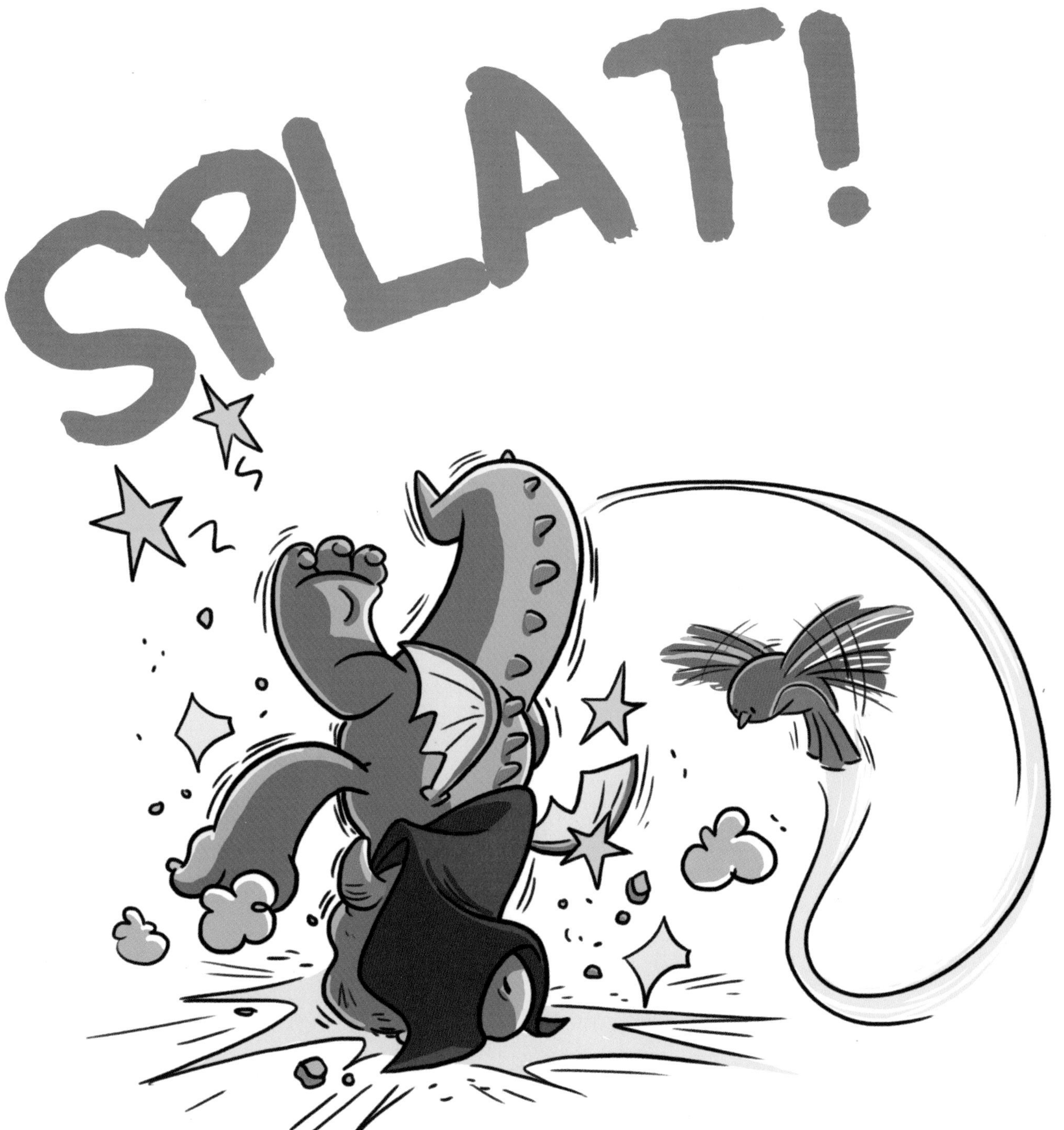
SPLAT!

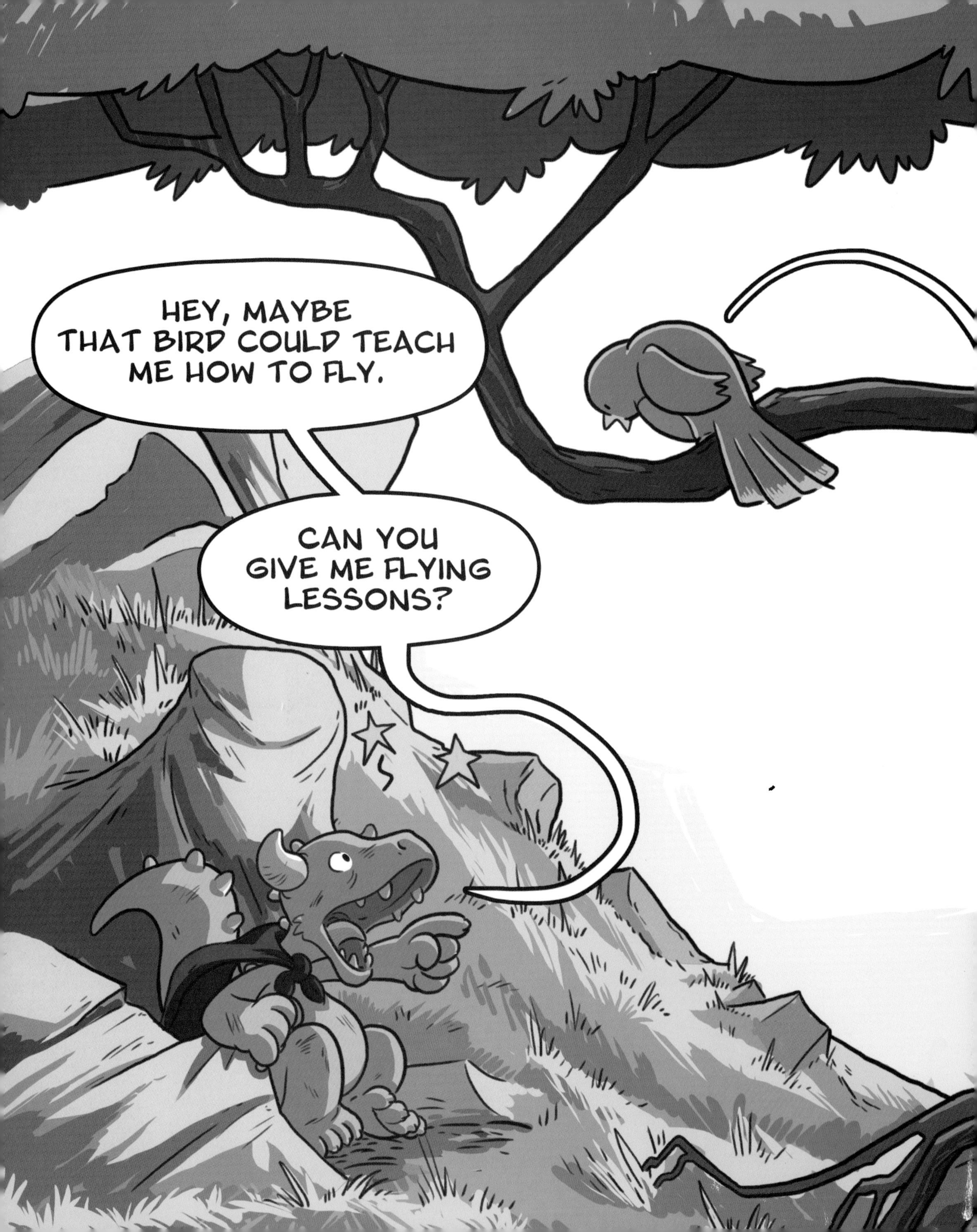
HEY, MAYBE THAT BIRD COULD TEACH ME HOW TO FLY.
CAN YOU GIVE ME FLYING LESSONS?

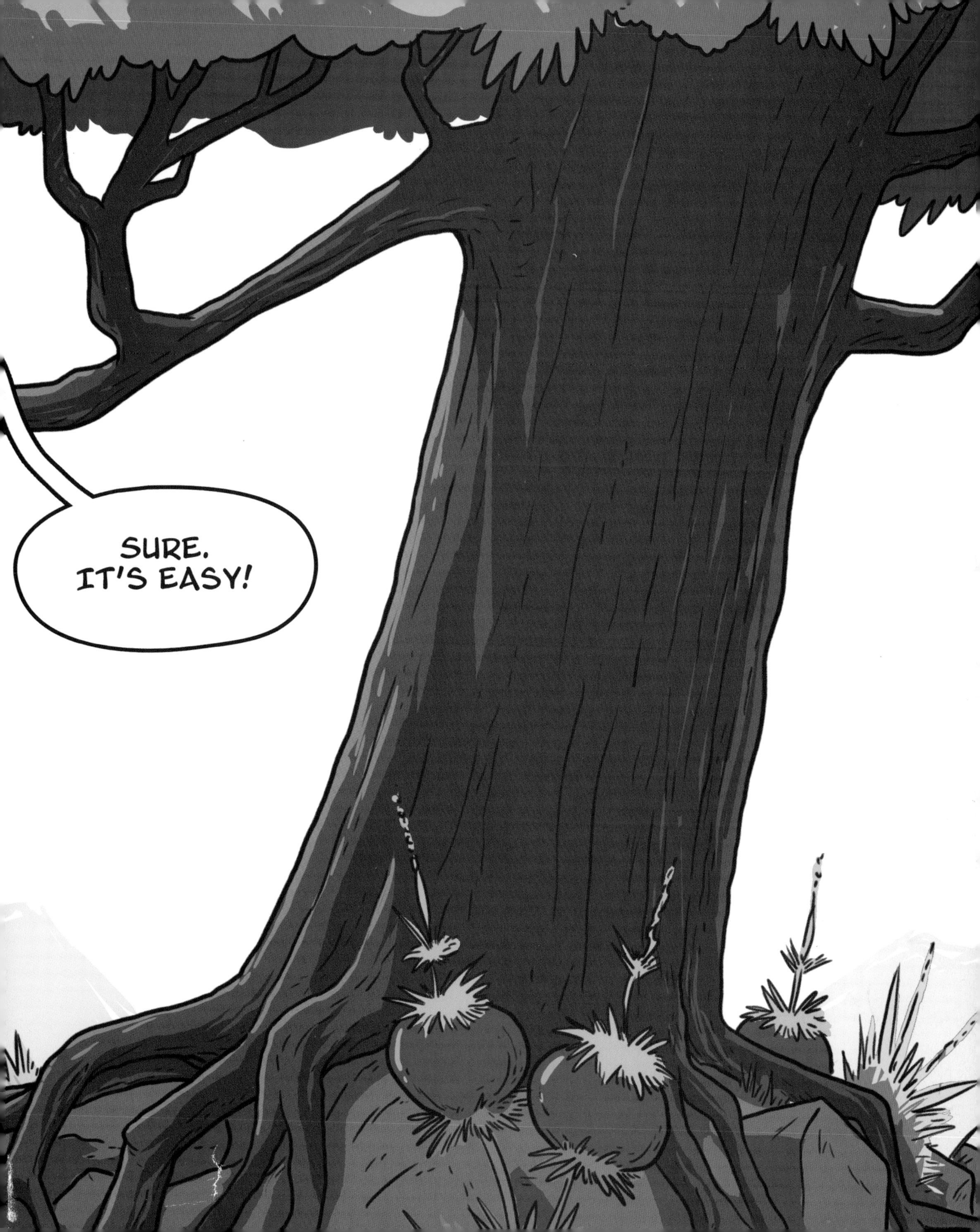
SURE. IT'S EASY!

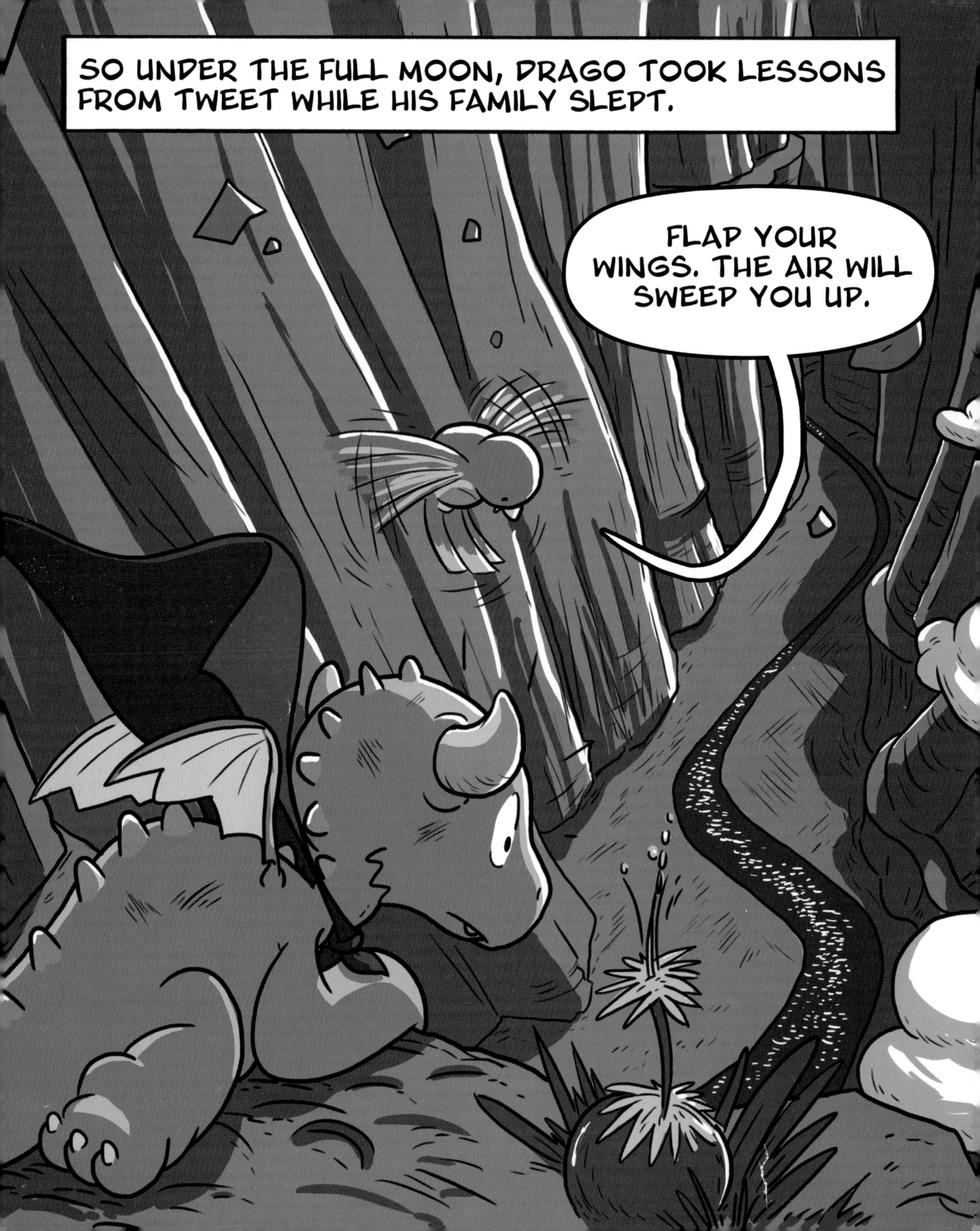
SO UNDER THE FULL MOON, DRAGO TOOK LESSONS FROM TWEET WHILE HIS FAMILY SLEPT.
FLAP YOUR WINGS. THE AIR WILL SWEEP YOU UP.

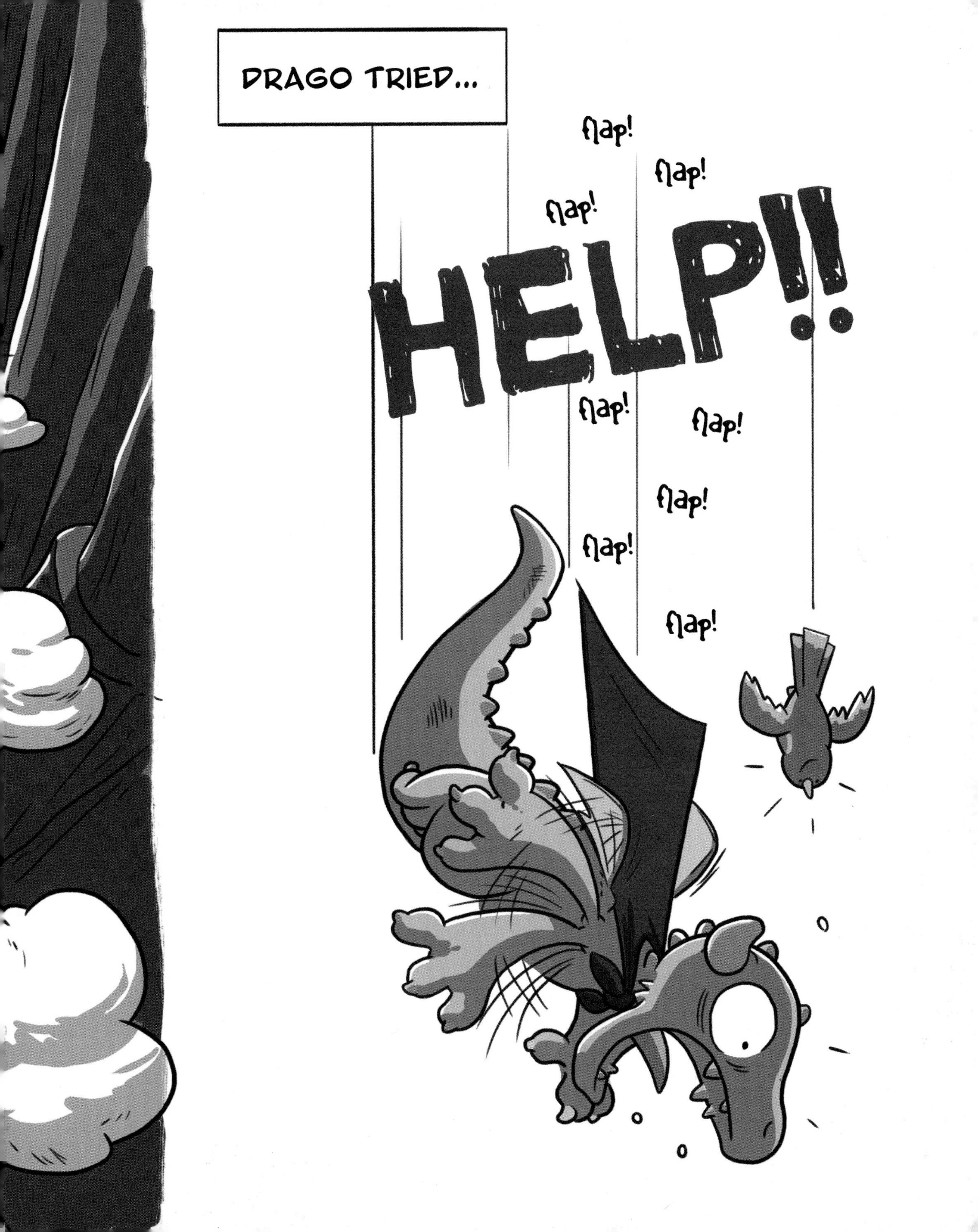
DRAGO TRIED...
flap!
flap!
flap!
HELP!!
flap!
flap!
flap!
flap!
flap!

AND TRIED AGAIN...

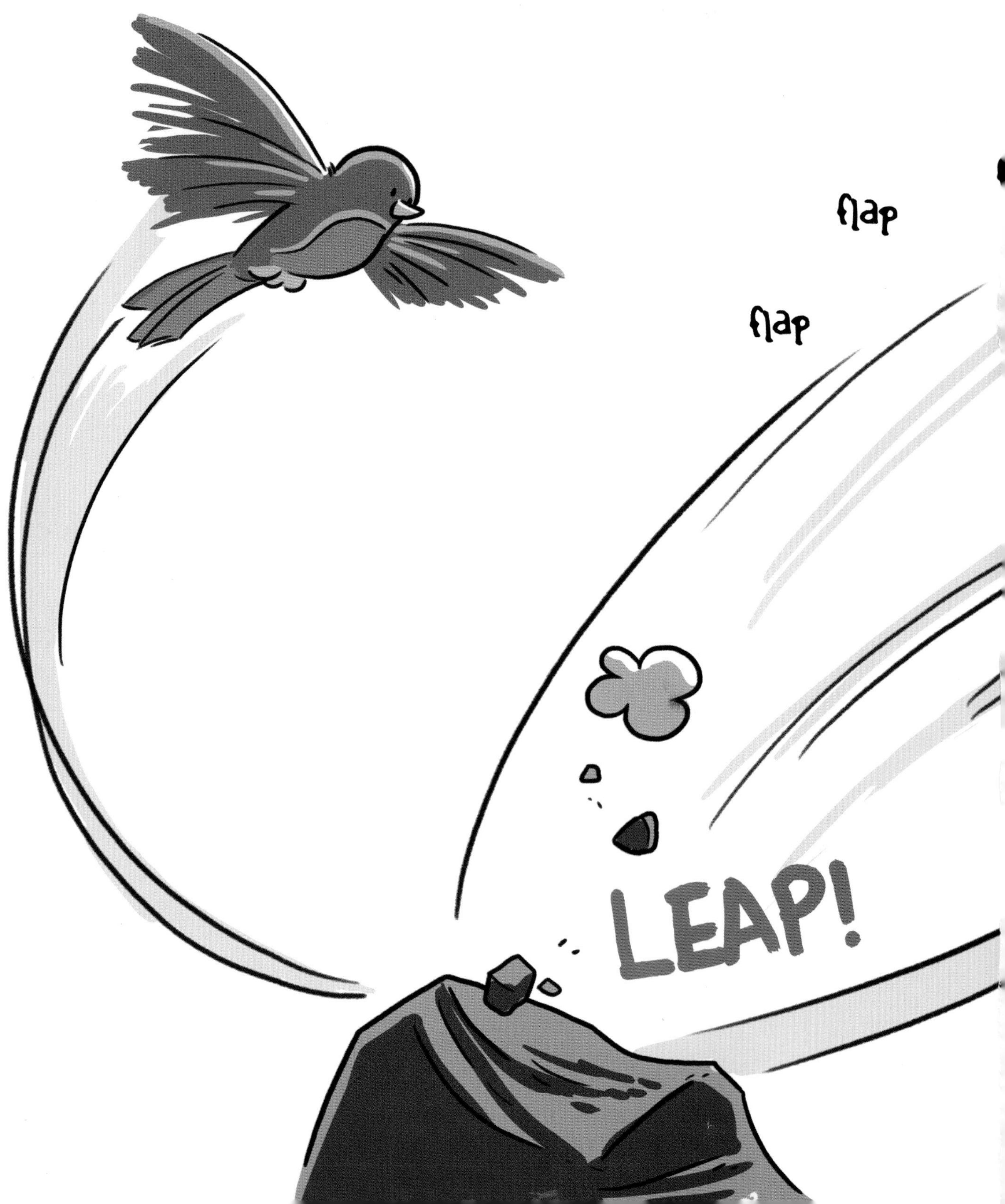
flap
flap
LEAP!

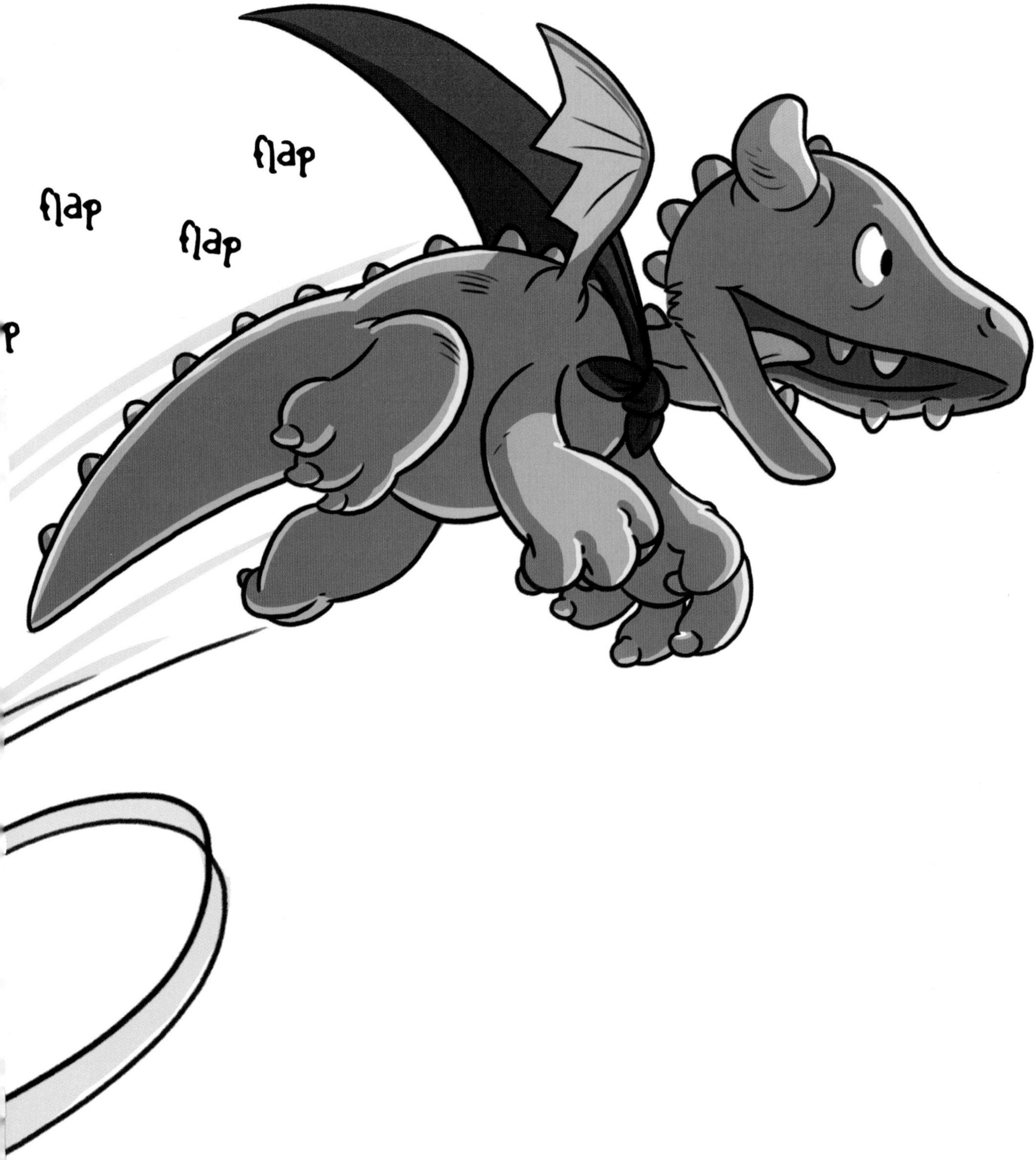
flap
flap
flap

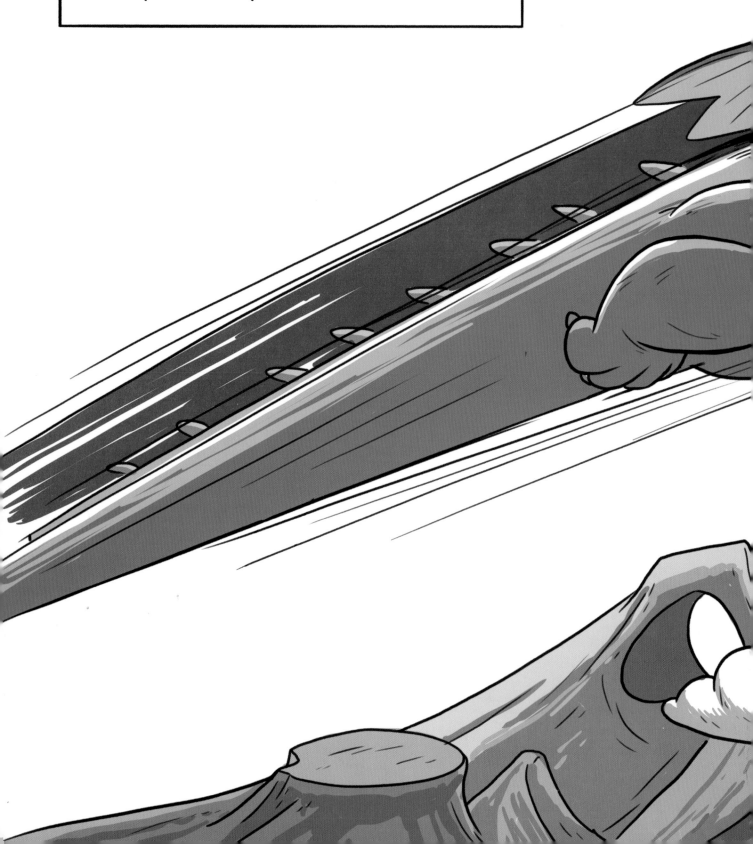

UNTIL, FINALLY, DRAGO WAS FLYING!

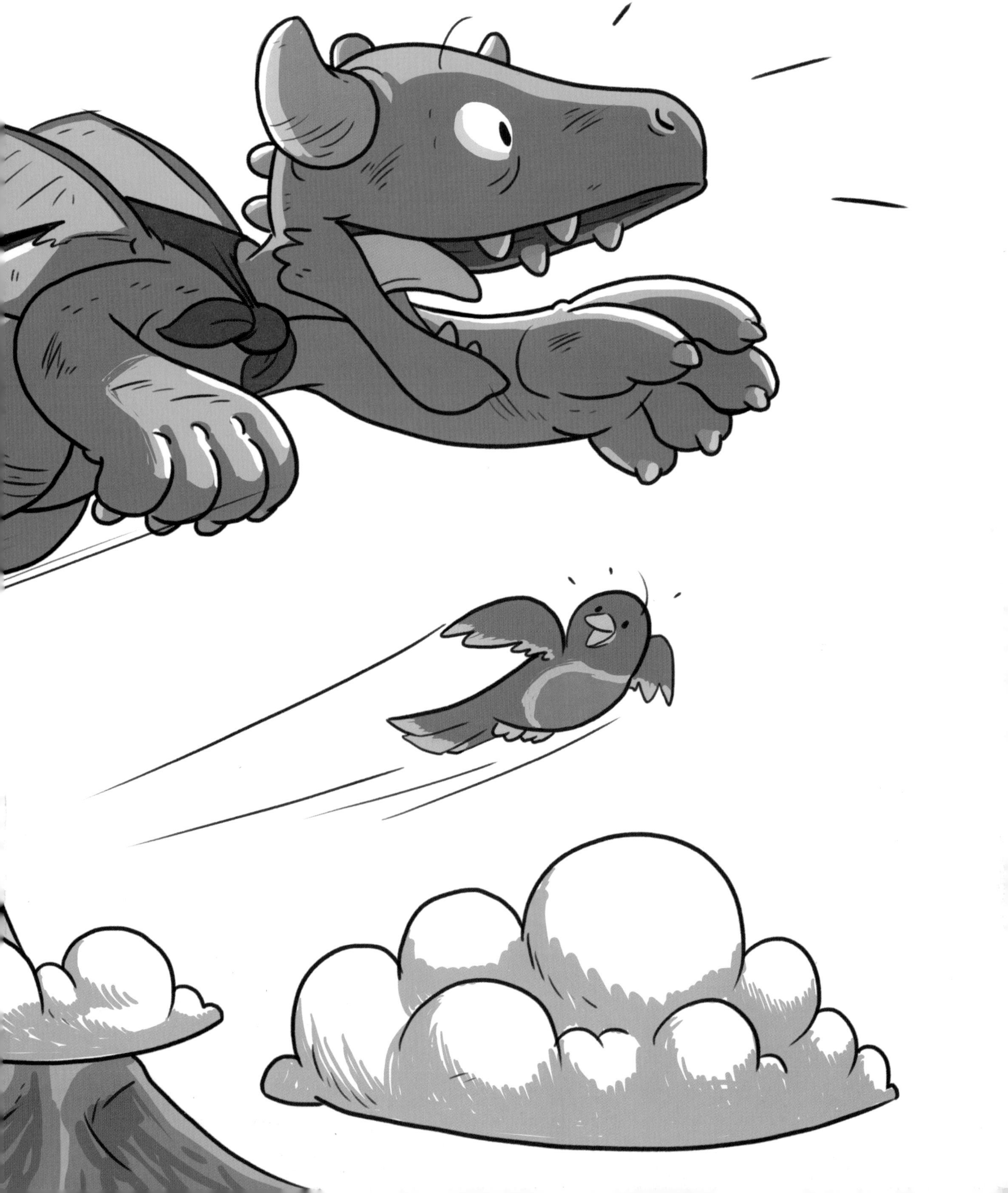

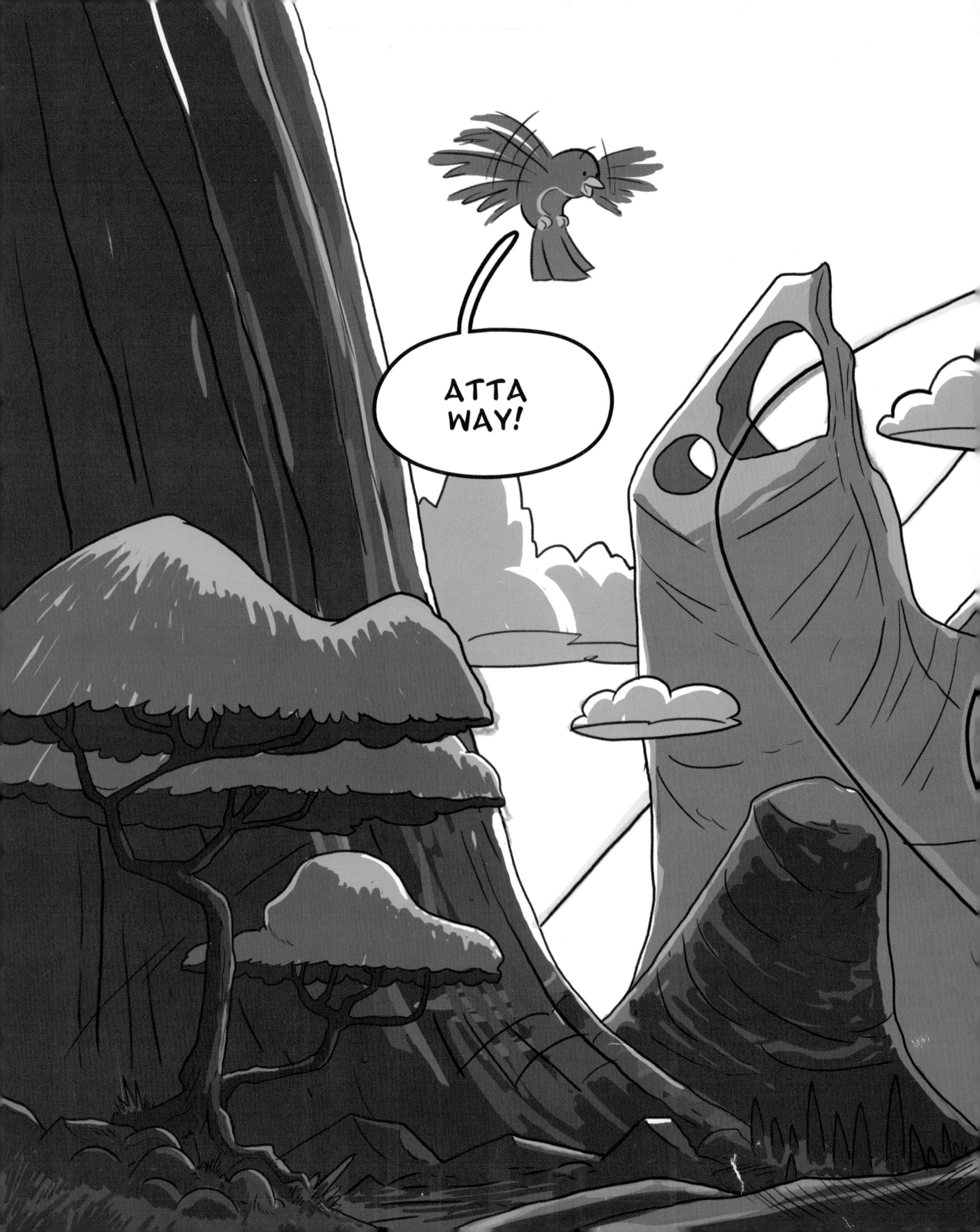
ATTA WAY!

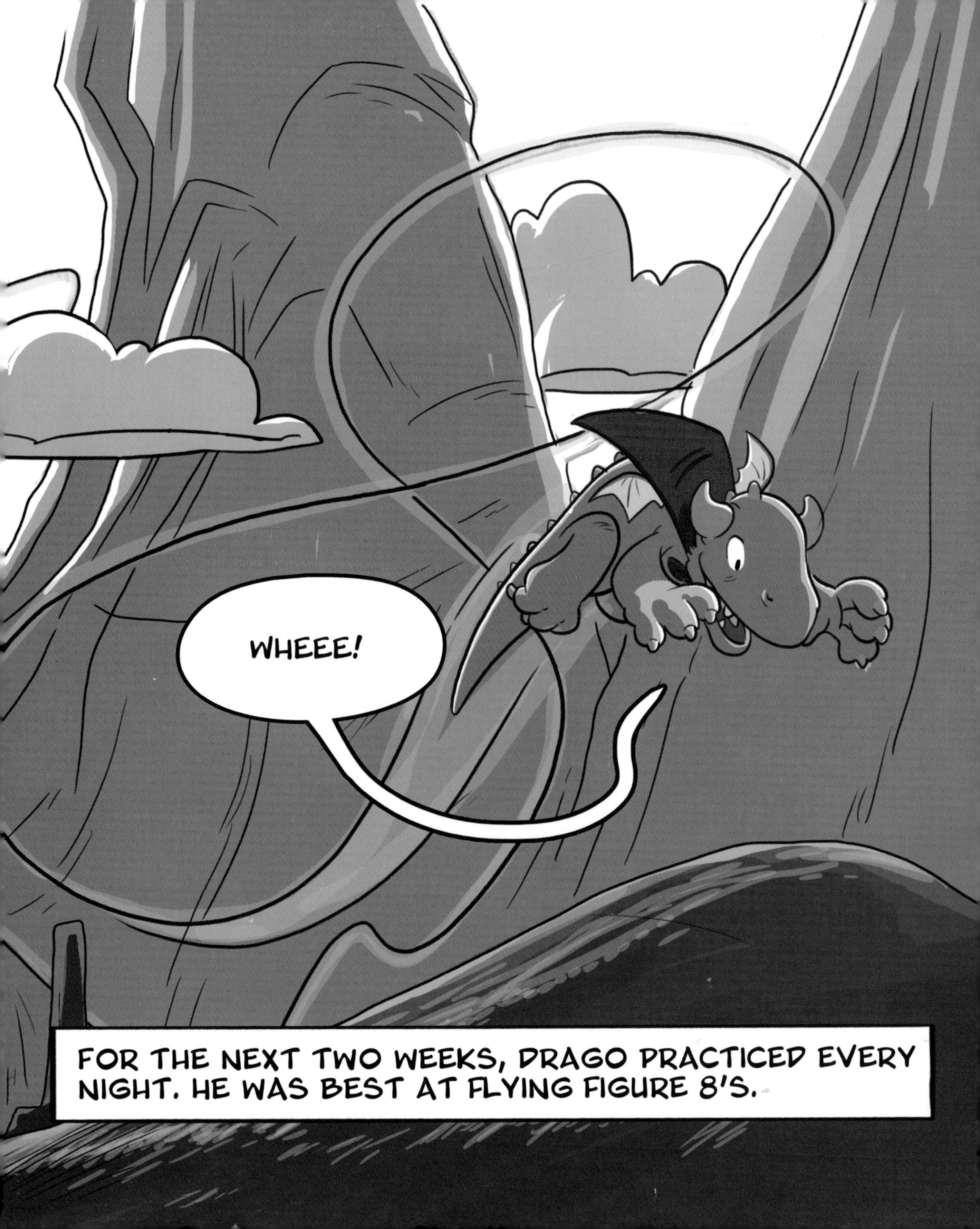
WHEEE!
FOR THE NEXT TWO WEEKS, DRAGO PRACTICED EVERY NIGHT. HE WAS BEST AT FLYING FIGURE 8'S.

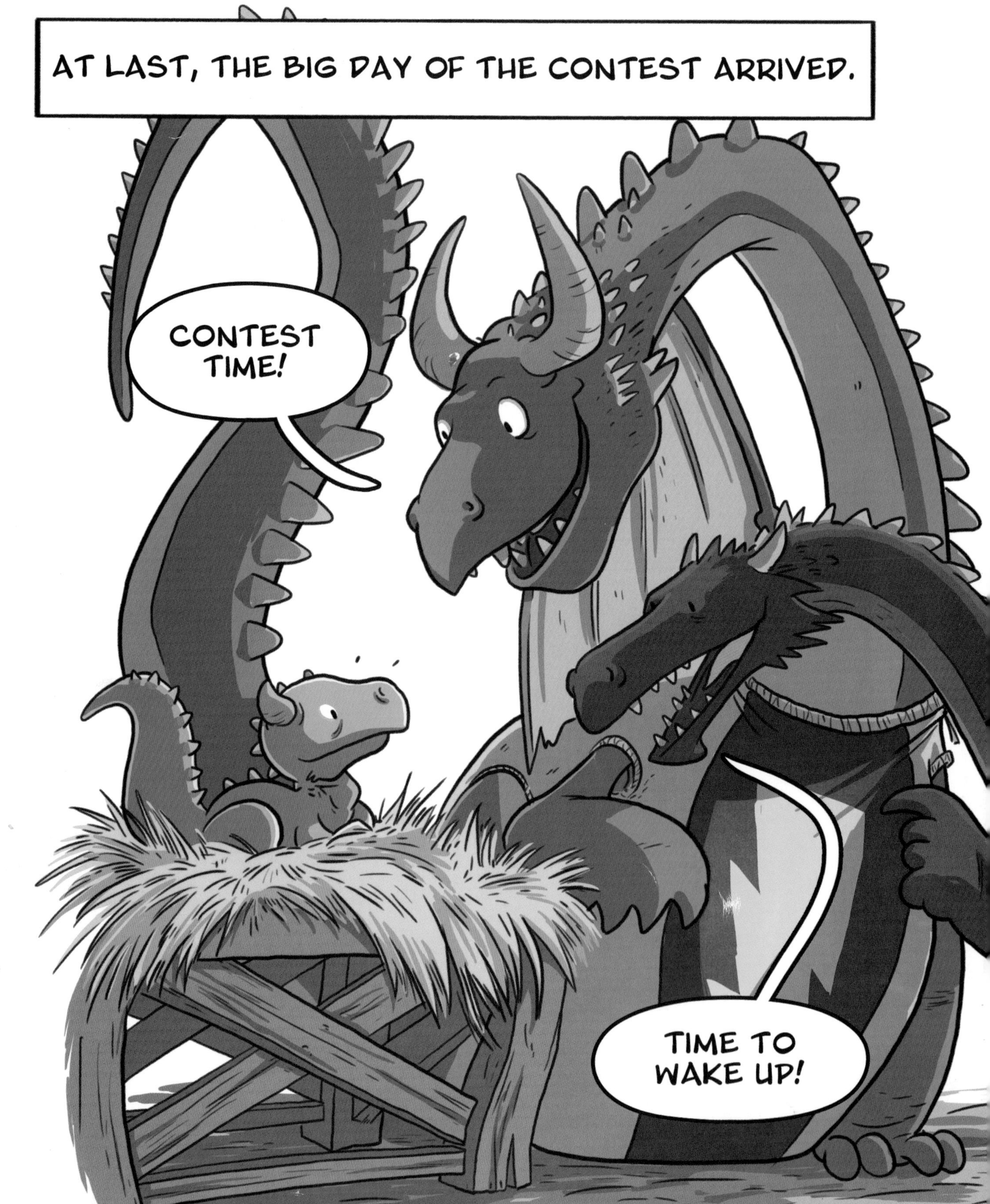
AT LAST, THE BIG DAY OF THE CONTEST ARRIVED.
CONTEST TIME!
TIME TO WAKE UP!

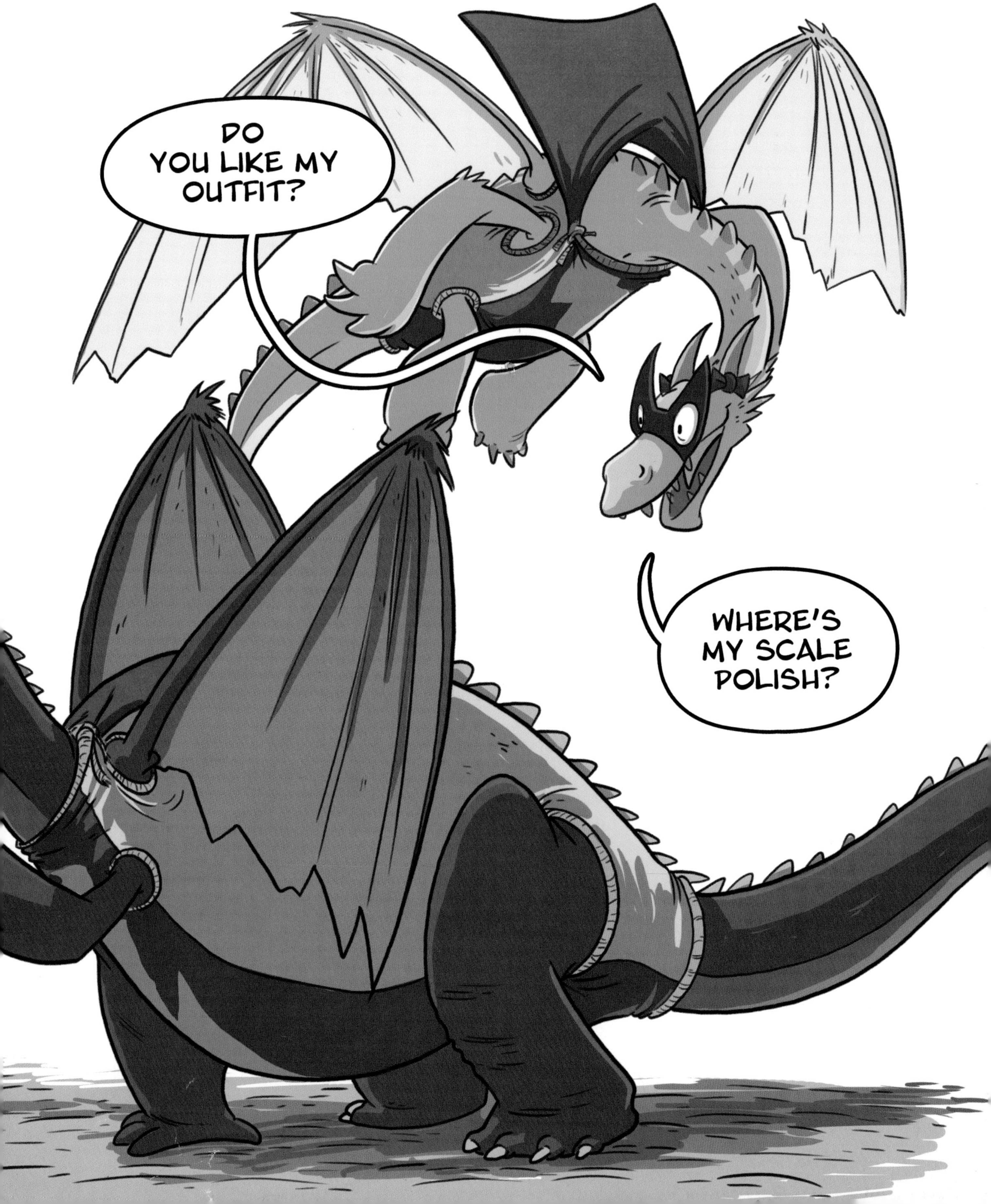
DO YOU LIKE MY OUTFIT?
WHERE'S MY SCALE POLISH?

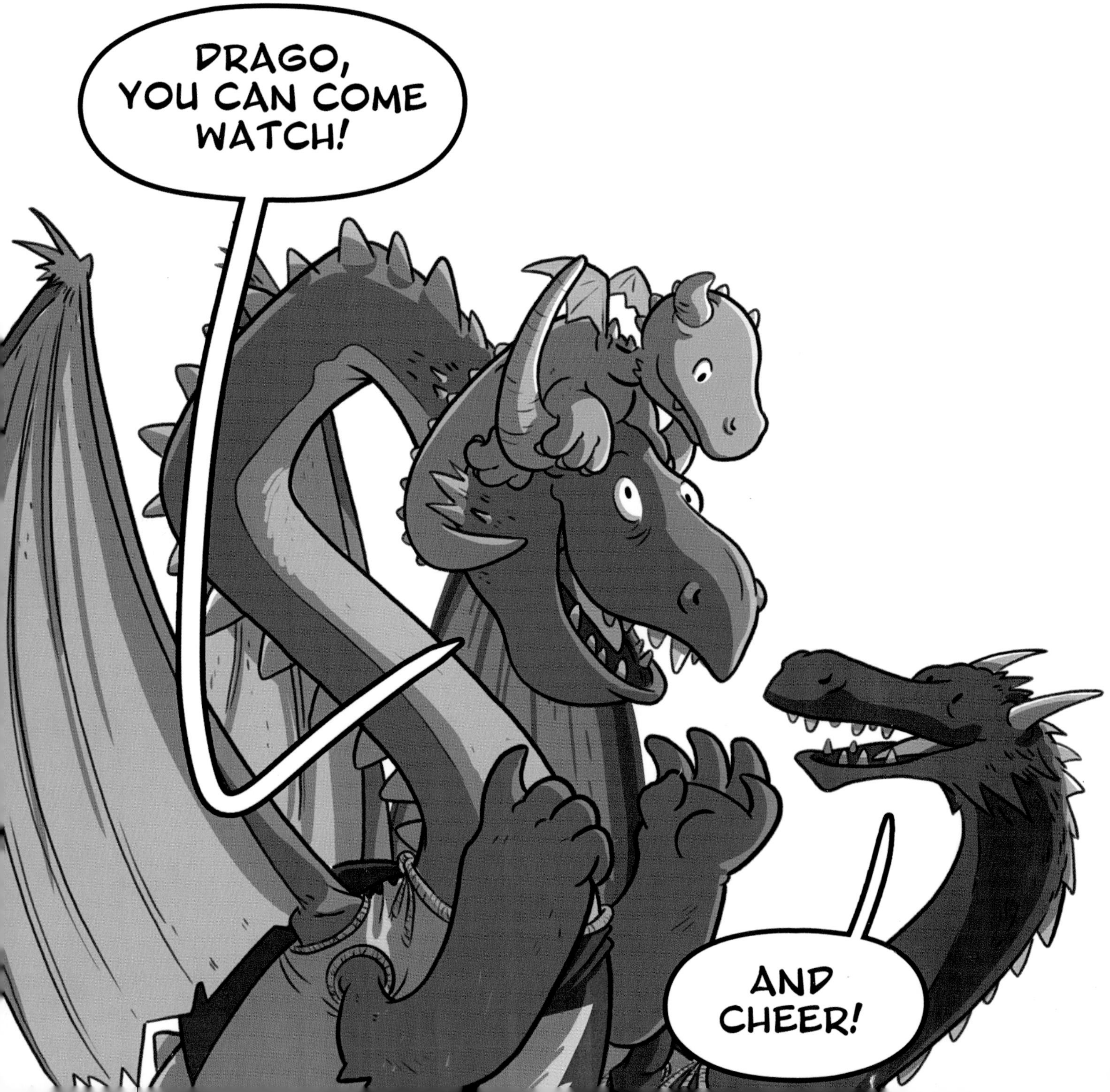
DRAGO, YOU CAN COME WATCH!
AND CHEER!

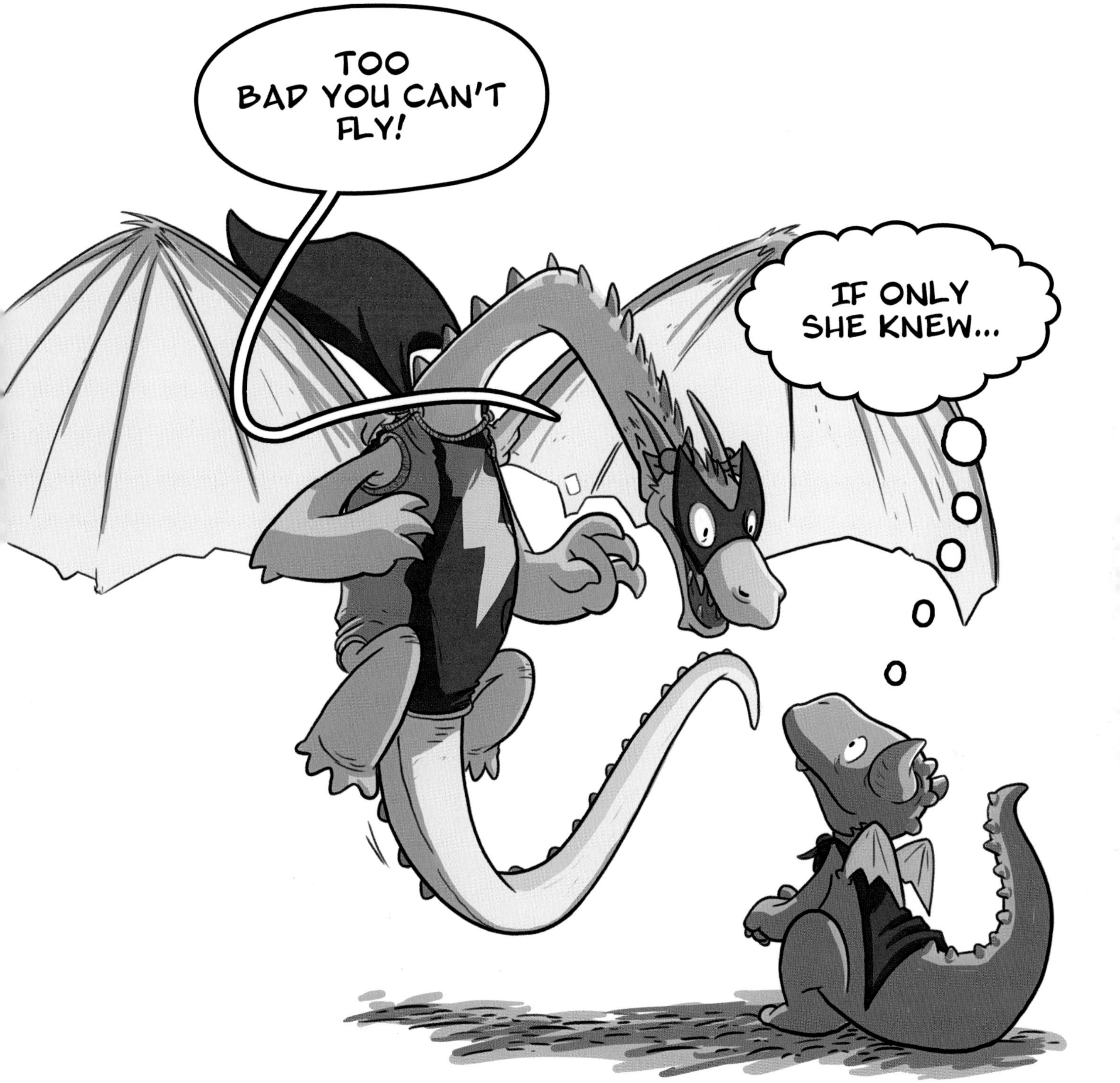
TOO BAD YOU CAN'T FLY!
IF ONLY SHE KNEW...

DRAGO RODE TO THE CONTEST
WITH HIS FATHER.

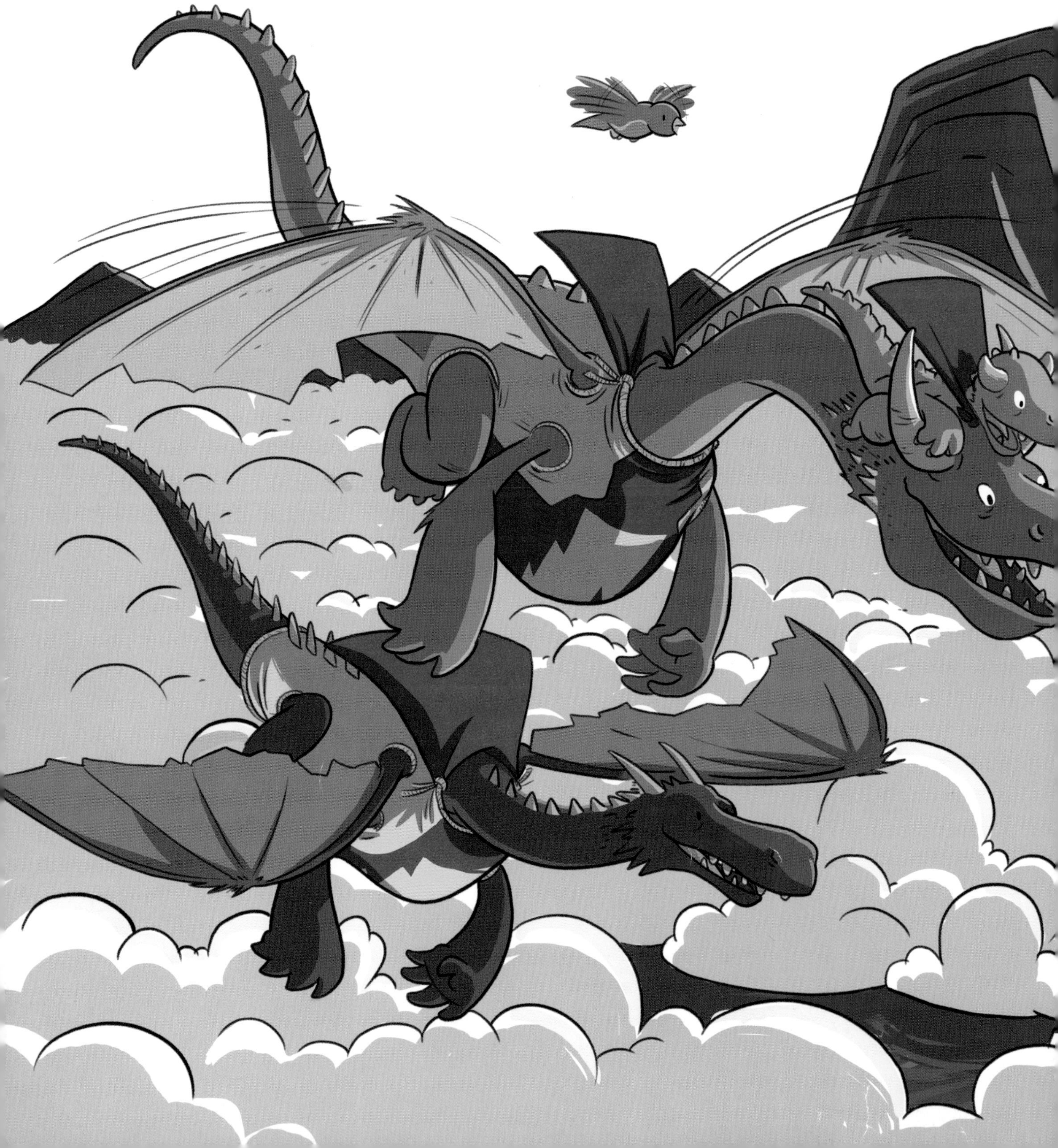

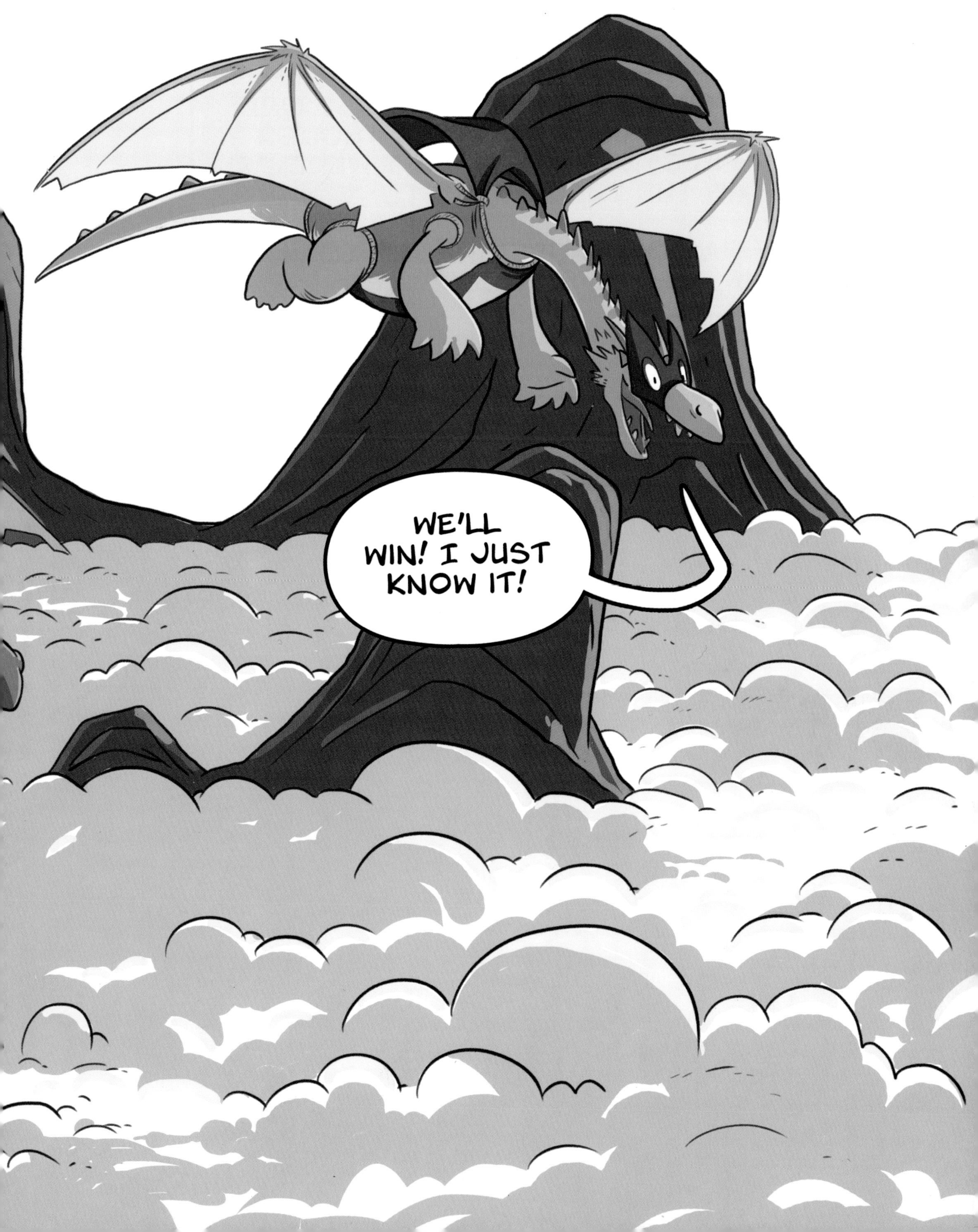
WE'LL WIN! I JUST KNOW IT!

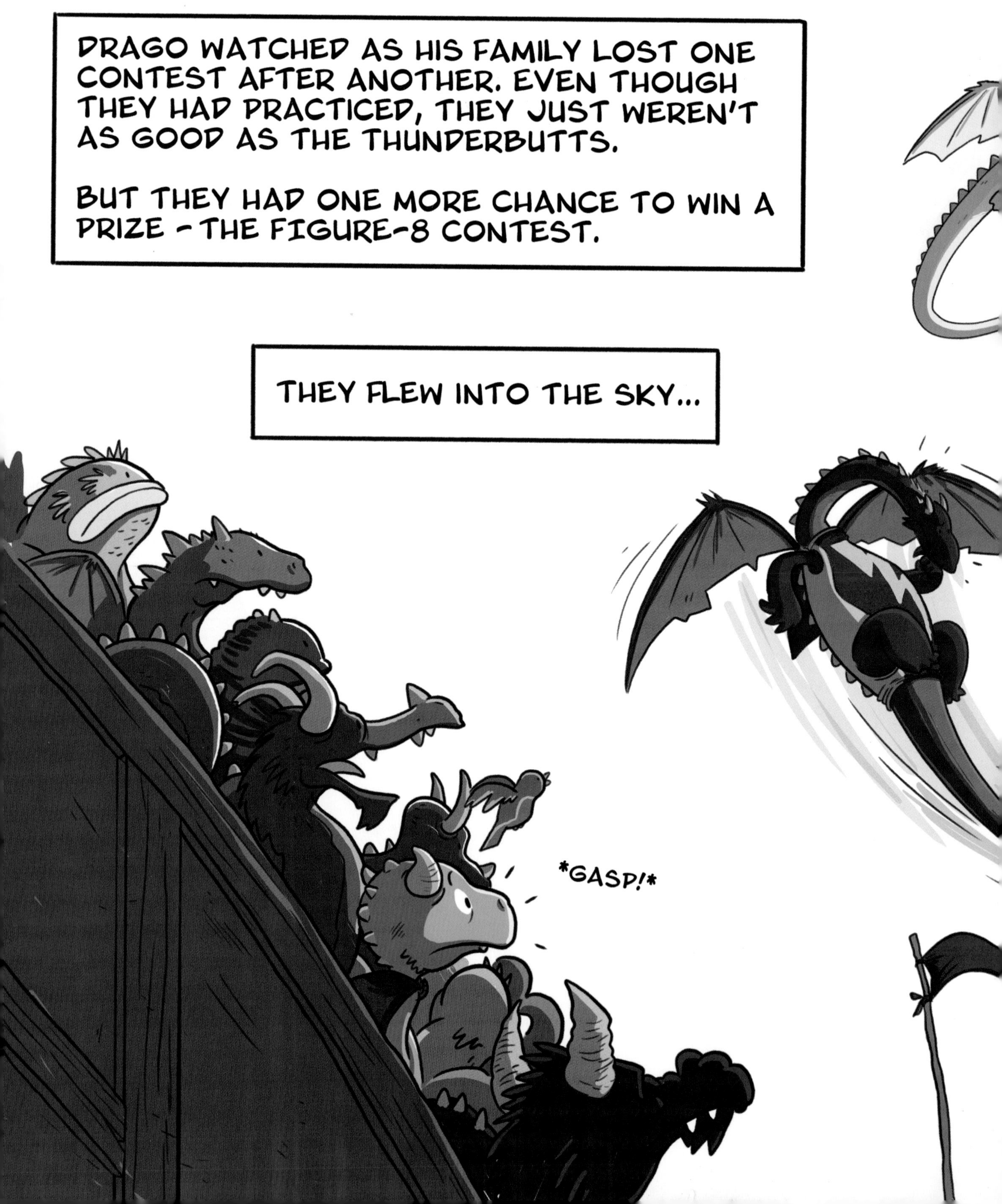
DRAGO WATCHED AS HIS FAMILY LOST ONE CONTEST AFTER ANOTHER. EVEN THOUGH THEY HAD PRACTICED, THEY JUST WEREN'T AS GOOD AS THE THUNDERBUTTS.
BUT THEY HAD ONE MORE CHANCE TO WIN A PRIZE - THE FIGURE-8 CONTEST.
THEY FLEW INTO THE SKY...
GASP!

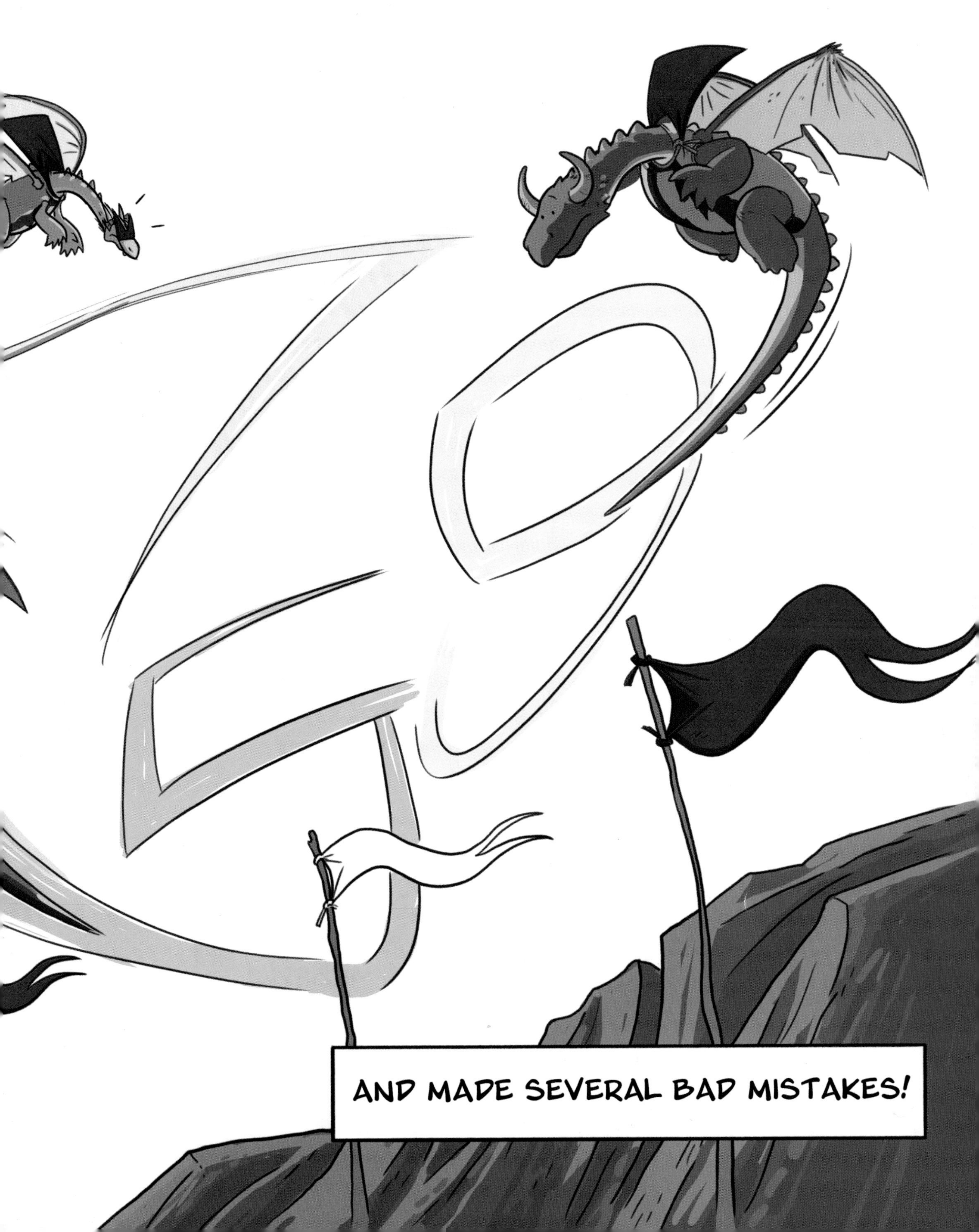
AND MADE SEVERAL BAD MISTAKES!

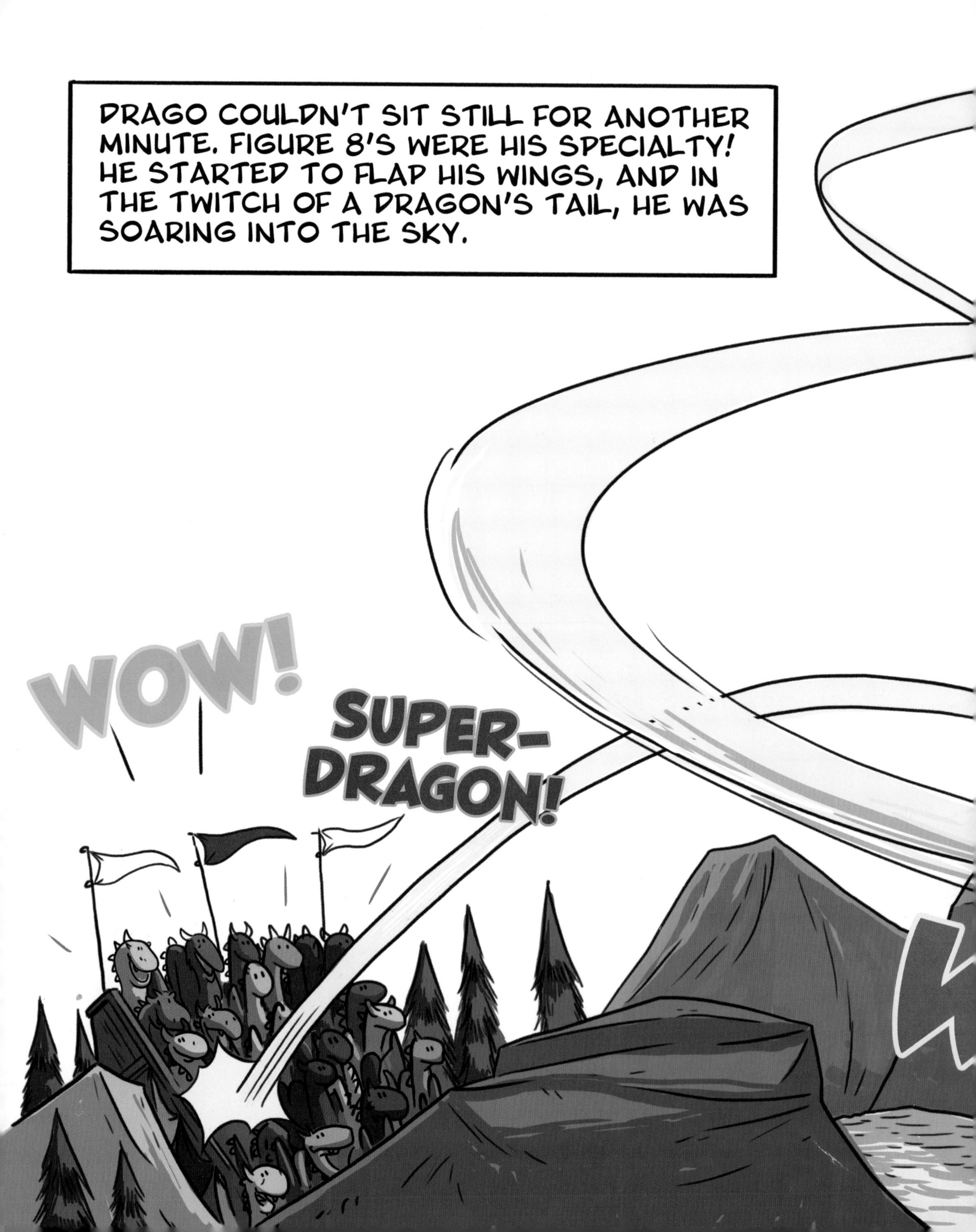
DRAGO COULDN'T SIT STILL FOR ANOTHER MINUTE. FIGURE 8'S WERE HIS SPECIALTY! HE STARTED TO FLAP HIS WINGS, AND IN THE TWITCH OF A DRAGON'S TAIL, HE WAS SOARING INTO THE SKY.
WOW!
SUPER-DRAGON!

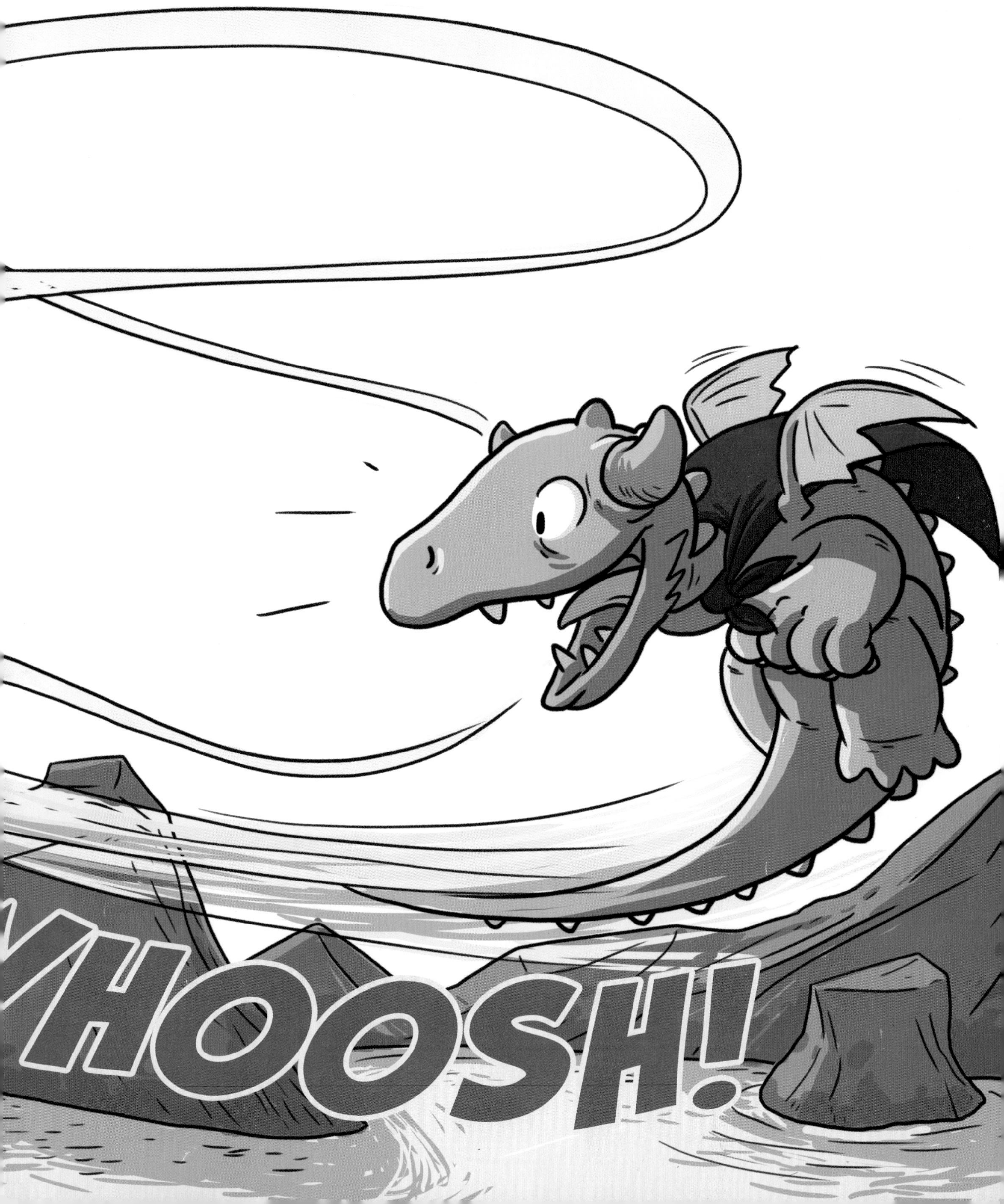

WHOOSH!

MUCH TO HIS FAMILY'S AMAZEMENT, DRAGO WON FIRST PRIZE, A BRAND-NEW DRAGON'S BREATH FIRE EXTINGUISHER AND $25!!!

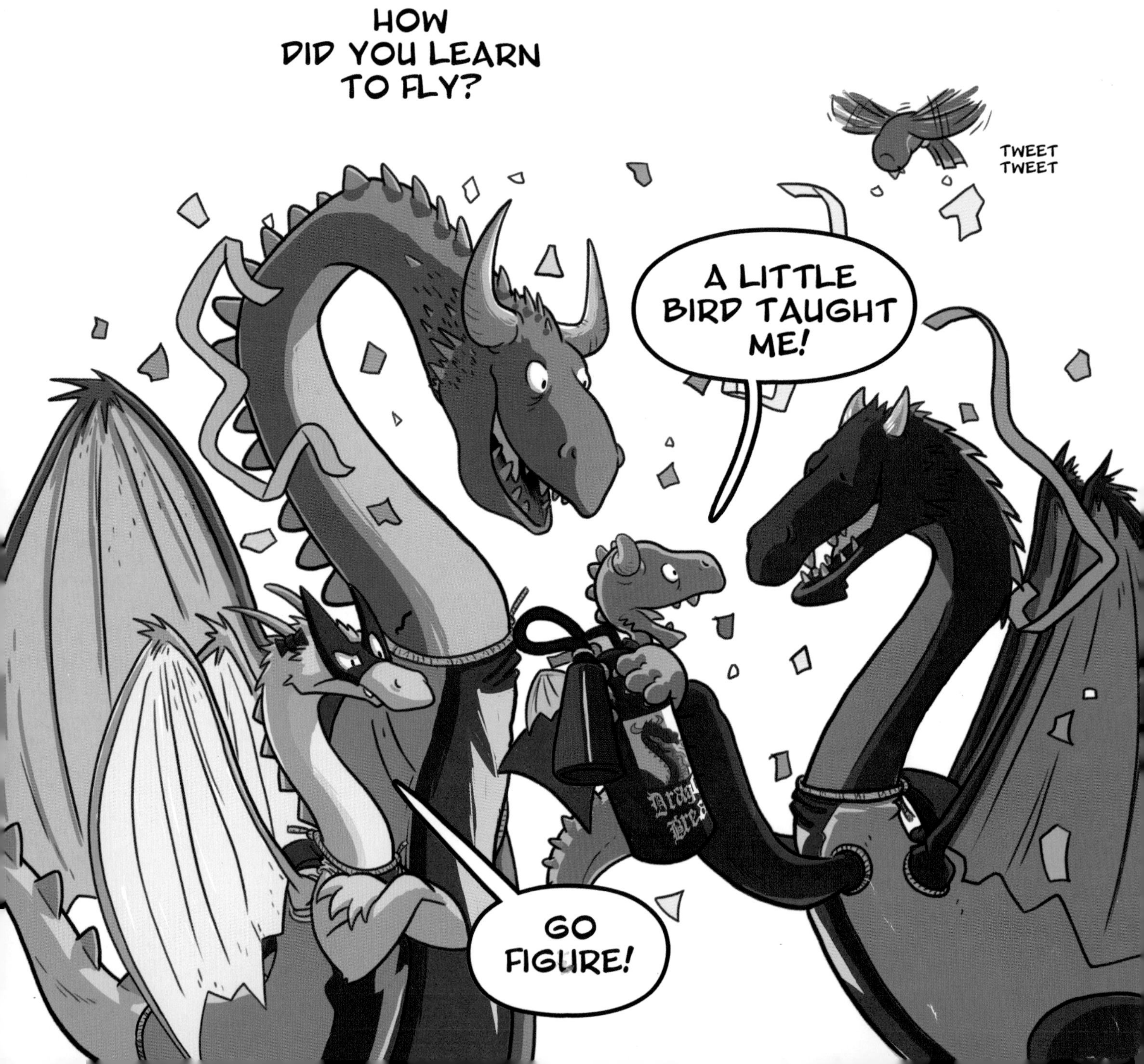
HOW DID YOU LEARN TO FLY?
TWEET TWEET
A LITTLE BIRD TAUGHT ME!
GO FIGURE!